BEYOND THE FENCE

A SHORT COLLECTION OF STORIES

MARILYN HORN

Thinking Ink Press

Campbell, California

Praise for Beyond the Fence

"Marilyn Horn creates worlds that merge the strangeness of fantasy with deep compassion and strength of humanity—predominantly seen through her female characters who leave you soul-searching yet grounded in certainty. Horn brilliantly takes us *Beyond the Fence* and even further than the stratosphere."

—Julie Demoff-Larson, *Blotterature Literary Magazine*

"Traversing the rolling hills of Marilyn Horn's imagination is both soothing and eerily distracting. Each story is like sipping on a cool drink in the summertime only to be knocked in the chest by a surprising, though pleasant, after-taste. These could be distant, though wiser and healthier relatives of the Binewskis from Katherine Dunn's *Geek Love*. But they live on the slightly saner side of the hill.
A fine, cohesive collection from an original voice."

—Parthenia M. Hicks, Poet Laureate Emerita, Los Gatos, California

"Marilyn's stories combine the earthy and the mystical. Within these pages, you'll meet a rollicking cast of heart-filled and hope-challenged characters you won't soon forget. The symbolism will stay with you long after you close the cover, and it will invite you back in for a second read. These are stories not to be missed."

—Melanie Faith, MFA, creative writing instructor at WOW! Women on Writing and adjunct English professor at Southern New Hampshire University graduate school

Published by Thinking Ink Press
P.O. Box 1411, Campbell, California, 95009
Second printing, 2016

ISBN 978-1-942480-15-0

Printed in the United States of America.

Project Credits

Cover art: Sandi Billingsley

Cover concept: Keiko O'Leary

Cover design: Keri Knutson

Editor: Keiko O'Leary

Interior layout: Betsy Miller

Contents

Foreword

In this marvelous chapbook from Marilyn Horn, a writer friend I've been happy to know for years now, you will find tenderness and wonder, siblings and Jupiter, a mobile made of armadillo bones, Forever Trees and soul genes, a story-telling dolphin, and a monster for justice. Wisdom and a sweet quiet voice.

Unpredictable, these stories and characters will stick with you, accompany you on rainy mornings and foggy afternoons. Some are so short you can practically read them before the light turns green (not recommended), others in the time it takes to wait for a prescription. How lucky we are to have these gems threaded on one string, a portable collection. Perfect, as they say, for gifts, especially a gift to yourself.

> —Lita Kurth, co-founder, Flash Fiction Forum; creative writing instructor, De Anza College and private workshops

Return of the Son

Mary lives at the end of the garden path. She is my only friend these days. But what she said yesterday—I didn't like that. Perhaps we shouldn't discuss our sons. You know how it is, when mothers talk about their children. Sometimes things are said that shouldn't be. Once I find my cane, I'll go see Mary, and she and I will have a little chat. Perhaps then our friendship can be saved.

But where is my cane? Someone has hidden it. They hide things from me here. They never admit it, of course. They say instead, "No, dear, we didn't hide that. You never had one of those." That's their way of telling me I'm crazy. They all think that here.

Mary doesn't think I'm crazy—one more reason she's my only friend. But she shouldn't have said what she did. I seethed over it all night, pacing the halls, until the nurse took me back to my room and tied me to my bed.

I see my cane now: on top of the trunk. My son's trunk, below the window. Both cane and trunk are made of mahogany, which is why I couldn't see it before. The trunk takes up nearly the whole room, but I'll never part from it. My son will want it when he returns. My room here is too small, that's the problem. Not like my flat on Kensington Square. But at least it's sunny here, and I have a view of the garden, and the trees, and the hills beyond, crisscrossed with stone walls and dotted with sheep. "Such a grand view!" is what my son will say.

It was a sad day when his trunk arrived in Kensington. I cried as I sorted through his things—his helmet, his medals, the pistol they say he drew during that nasty battle …

My son would never charge a rapid-fire gun with only a pistol— such nonsense! Why do they lie to me so?

My husband lied to me, too. "Yes, yes, my love. He is only asleep," my husband said, but he didn't believe it. He's the one who sent me here.

Mary understands my dilemma, or at least I thought she did. "It is our burden to bear, knowing what we know, and having such sons"—that's what she told me the first time we met. But now her heart has turned from me. Why else would she say such awful things? Why say "My son never …" Oh, I can't bear to think of it.

Cane in hand, I leave my room. I hobble down the long white corridor, past the orderlies who reek of cigarettes, past the fat nurses in their stiff starched dresses. All in white, as if they are angels. But they aren't. They watch me as I pass. They are always watching me. The doctor is the one I hate the most, with his oiled hair and sour breath. He says terrible things to me when he visits my room. "The Somme" and "no-man's land"—those are the words I hate the most. I cover my ears when he says them.

Outside, the clouds are low, and the air is cool, thick and moist, making everything muted—the bird song, the colors of the flowers, even the crunch of the gravel path. "Off to see Mary, are we?" It's the gardener who asks me this, a pip of a man with broken teeth and one blind eye. I don't answer him. He knows—everyone knows— that I visit Mary every day.

It would not be right, not fitting, for her to visit me, and so neither she nor I mention it. We speak only of our sons. She is waiting for hers to return; poor thing, she has been waiting all these years. I am waiting as well, of course, but I will not have so long to wait.

Still, it's been ages since I saw him last. So handsome in his uniform, a grown man for all to see, and yet still my little boy. My baby. The youngest of my six children. The strongest and healthiest of them all, and the only one left to me, all the others dying so long ago. Even that day at the train station, as he stood there in his uniform, I saw my little boy, with his ruddy cheeks, his unruly hair, his eyes bright with mischief. "I've brought you a gift, Mummy," he'd say when he was small, after an excursion to the park, and from behind his back he'd reveal a toad, or a lizard, or—sometimes—a flower. Violets, mostly. Such tiny things, so delicate.

Violets grow here, too, along the garden path, and there at the end of it stands Mary. Her face is pearled white, as are her hands, but her hooded robe is blue—the softest of blues, like a robin's egg. Her head is bowed. She is gazing at the red and purple primroses growing at her feet. Such a supplicant stance; so innocent, as if dreadful words have never passed her lips.

Mary smiles. She is always so happy to see me. I smile, too, and for a moment I forget I'm angry with her. But it doesn't last. "I was thinking of what you said, dear," I say as I approach. "It wasn't very nice."

Mary smiles. Says nothing.

"Did you hear me? I didn't like it. Not at all."

She doesn't answer at first. But then, her head still bowed, she says the same awful thing she said yesterday.

"My son never woke up."

I put my hands to my ears but can't block out her words.

"He never returned."

Such a hateful thing to say! And still she smiles that awful smile. *Your son won't return, either*—that is what her smile means, as if it is all some terrible joke, this waiting of ours. She's no better than the doctors or the orderlies or the hateful nurses. She's no better than my husband.

I strike her with my cane. I strike her again and again. I am not so old and feeble after all! I make a small chink on her nose, and yet still she smiles.

The gardener is soon there, and he takes my cane. Then there are others—two young men, both in white. Young men, my son's age. I search their faces, but they are only orderlies. My son is not among them. He is still asleep in France.

They hold my arms. They drag me away, and my slippered feet scrape over the graveled path.

"Liar!" I yell at Mary. "Liar!"

My son will return to me.

No matter what Mary says.

Don't Mind the Vet

The mobile made of armadillo bones rattled in the stiff cold breeze at the window. Bettina looked past it to the dirt hills dotted with sage brush, silver with frost. Cold morning outside, but hot in here, even with the window partly open, the mesquite logs in the small fireplace filling the whole house with their sweet warmth.

"In English, Meyma," Bettina said again, careful not to sound impudent. This was her mother, after all. "Please say in English."

Her mother lay pale and listless on her narrow bed. She sighed and said, "For Chico sake, don't mind the vet."

Bettina moved her chair closer to the bed and felt her mother's brow. "Meyma, what you—what do you mean, 'Don't mind the vet'?"

Chico the Chihuahua watched Bettina from his spot atop Meyma's stomach. Meyma stroked his little black ears with her thumb and finger and shook her head. *"Eku nu eku nu."*

"You know I don't speak the old words anymore. English, Meyma. English."

Meyma turned her face away from Bettina, a gesture that meant the words would pain her to say. Bettina sat up straight in her little chair, extra alert.

"The eyes see what they see," Meyma said. "Don't mind the vet. Nothing more to say."

Meyma talking in riddles, the way she had always done, like everyone here in town did. Not saying anything point blank, not like in San Antonio, where Bettina lived now, and had lived these past 10 years. In San Antonio, if you said, "I'll have the lemon-butter grilled salmon and a glass of Pinot Noir," that is what you meant, and that is what you got.

"Fine. Fine. I won't mind the vet," Bettina said and then muttered, before she could stop herself, "not even if he puts a goat in my attic." Meyma smiled at her use of the old phrase, but Bettina pretended not to notice. "But it's you who should see the doctor, not this dog. He's just sick because you don't feel good." Chico looked up at her with sad kind eyes and Bettina softened her tone. "Or maybe you're just not feeding him right." This morning he had spit up ugly chunks of brown and red all over the straw rug.

Meyma shook her head. "I sick because he sick. Once he better, I be. How it works."

"Fine." Bettina checked her watch and got up to leave.

"You not wearing *that?*" Meyma said, her black eyes big and round. Scared.

Bettina looked down at her long-sleeved shirt, her slacks and boots. "Yes, why not?"

Meyma turned her face away. "Too much. Too much. Wear the blue blouse. In the closet."

Blue brought health, Bettina knew that. Or that is what Meyma believed, anyway. "It's too cold to wear that," she said and then added, when Meyma still looked perplexed, "I'm wearing a blue bra. Don't worry."

She bundled up the dog in an old woven blanket and walked down the hard-dirt road toward the vet's office. The sooner Meyma got to feeling better, the sooner Bettina could go home. Back to San Antonio. Away from this cold dust hole 500 miles from anywhere.

Back to her real life, back to her friends—the ones who glittered sharp and brilliant and piercing, like the bleached bones the townspeople here hung in windows to ward off evil. If getting back home meant taking Chico to the vet, then she would do it.

In the vet's waiting room, a nurse with a long white braid sat reading a paperback. She took notice of Bettina and pointed her to an empty seat and went back to her reading.

Chico snuggled into the crook of Bettina's arm and peeked out at the other women filling the room, coddling their dogs and their cats. All women, Bettina noticed. No men. Women she had seen throughout her growing-up years, coming down from the hills for the bonfires and the festivals. All women here, and all wearing such low-cut blouses. "*Ay ko!*" Poppy would have said, back in the day, for he had always admired the feminine form. None of them younger than 60, as far as Bettina could tell, and all showing their cleavage. Wearing blouses like she had found hanging in her mother's closet. Like the blue one Meyma had wanted her to wear.

Bettina ran her fingers up the long line of buttons on her long-sleeved shirt. Even the top one was buttoned. Her friends in San Antonio wore shirts like this. Stiff and starched, like something a man might wear.

The woman sitting next to Bettina had a broad brown face and long gray-black hair and held a despondent Pomeranian on her lap. "You're Evie's daughter," she said and grinned, revealing a mouth of silver teeth ("Such a mouth means luck and wisdom"—another thing Poppy would have said). "How she be?"

"Not as well as can be." An expression Bettina hadn't used in years, and yet it fell easily from her lips, like fluff from a cottonwood.

"And little dog worries about her," the woman said. "Poor little dog. Your meyma's best friend all these years, since your poppy passed." The woman kissed the tips of fingers when she said it. Bettina nearly performed the ritual, too, but held herself in check.

"She tell you about the vet?" The woman inclined her head toward the closed door of the examination room.

"She told me not to mind the vet. What she—what did she mean?"

The woman smiled knowingly. "*Ay keke.* Let's say he not look you in the eye." She readjusted the neckline of her blouse, revealing a worn and wrinkled cleavage.

Bettina noticed again all the low-cut blouses in the room and felt a pang of panic. Her hand went up to the buttons at the top of her neck. "You mean ..."

"Just let him look." The woman readjusted her neckline again. "He a miracle worker. He need inspiration. Everyone know that." She nodded to the other women in the waiting room and they responded in kind. "So don't mind the vet. For little dog sake. And your meyma."

Not mind? Bettina didn't know how she could *not* mind. And her friends back in the city—how disgusted they would be! Just like when Bettina told them about the wintertime bonfire, and how the snakes sizzled on the fire. "Sounds ghastly," they said, their voices clinking like champagne glasses, and after that she didn't talk about home. Not even her favorite things. The flower parade. The salamander dance.

If she listened hard, she could just make out what the vet said to each woman who entered the exam room. "They are as shy as two bunnies," she heard him say, and later, "They remind me of flying ducks." With each pronouncement, Bettina's hand flew to the buttons at her throat. More than once she got up to leave but sat right back down again, for Meyma's sake. Word would get back to Meyma that she had left without seeing the vet, and Meyma would cry. Not get angry, but cry. And that was worse.

But that was not the only reason Bettina stayed. Maybe, she thought, the vet really could cure the dog. She had seen such things before, on her very own body. The warts that fell off like scabs. The earaches and stomachaches, gone in a flash. All from the touch of sacred hands. If the vet could heal Chico, then Meyma would get better. And Bettina could go home.

The door to the exam room opened, and the nurse motioned to Bettina to go in. The woman with the silver teeth smiled encouragingly as Bettina crept toward the open door.

The vet was short and thin, brown and sun-parched, just like the desert sages who wandered into town on occasion, singing praises to the Old Mother. He looked at Bettina's buttoned-up shirt as she set the dog down on the examination table. His small brown eyes held a warmth and a depth Bettina had not seen in many years, and she felt safe with him, like she did with the old priest who had taught her the old prayers, even though the vet would not take his eyes from her chest. Chico looked up at her, pleading with her not to mind, while back at home, Bettina knew, her mother lay on the couch, awaiting good news.

"This is my mother's dog," she said and then quickly added, "I don't live here."

Chico looked from the vet to Bettina. The vet looked briefly at the dog and then stared again at Bettina's covered-up chest. Stared at the long column of buttons, each one tight in place. He frowned slightly and his shoulders seemed to sag.

"I don't live here," she said again.

They stood there for a long silent moment, the vet staring at her chest and Chico looking from one to the other. Finally Chico put his head down on his front paws and heaved a big sad sigh. "No can help little dog," the vet said, still staring at her chest, and he seemed like he would cry as he put his gnarled hand on the doorknob to let her out.

"Wait." Bettina looked deep into Chico's scared wet eyes and sighed. She undid the top button. And the next. And the next until they were all undone. And when the vet kept his hand on the doorknob, she undid the clasp of her little blue bra and pulled it down.

"They are like two healthy guinea pigs," he said, eyeing her breasts happily, unashamed, and he put a healing hand on the dog's stomach. And back at the house, Bettina saw it clear as day, Meyma got up to make a stew.

So Many Shoes

My project will never be complete.

So many shoes. I find them in abandoned homes and looted stores, and I bring them here to fill the sidewalks. In this way I can pretend I am not alone. These are not empty shoes scattered around me, I think. They are people. Mothers pushing trams. Businessmen making deals. Children skipping to the candy shop.

For a while I lined them up nicely, each shoe next to its match, but that looked to me as if the people had stopped in their tracks, which, if I am honest, is what happened. So many of them gone now, stopped forever. So I changed my tactic. I threw one shoe here, another there. Life seems fuller now. All these people I encounter as I wander the empty streets, they are slipshod, crazy, and completely human.

But, oh, so quiet.

A Big Gift

Past midnight, just as the planet Jupiter peeked from behind the old willow tree outside her window, Cassie heard Freddy stirring in the room next to hers, shifting and sighing, unable to get back to sleep. This was Cassie's cue, and she got out of bed and snuck downstairs to the dark kitchen. She prepared her big brother a bowl of corn flakes by the light of the moon, pouring just enough milk so that, when the cereal was gone, the milk would be nice and sweet.

She tiptoed carefully back up the stairs, the bowl big in her little hands, and found him sitting up in bed, the dim bedside lamp the only light in the room. Poor Freddy always looks so tired now, Cassie thought. His face was so pale compared with his black, black hair, but tonight it looked even paler, and his eyes were red-rimmed again, because he'd been crying. She had heard him earlier, when Mother had brought in the medicine.

She handed him the bowl before she climbed into bed next to him, and he slurped and crunched the cereal down without a spoon. "This is good," he said. He had hardly eaten anything all day. "My stomach hurts," was his usual excuse. No matter how much Mother threatened or begged, he ate hardly anything anymore, except the corn flakes Cassie brought him at night.

"You can start," he said. He handed her the empty bowl, and she put it on the nightstand and picked up the book, the one she had selected from the bookshelf in the room down the hall. Grandma's old room. The bookshelf there held dozens of books just like this one: *Our Wonderful Solar System.* She smoothed her hand over the book's shiny cover in an affectionate way, the way Grandma used to before opening it up.

"What chapter are we on?" He asked the same question every night.

"We're on the outer planets now," she said. They had finished the inner planets the night before. She opened up at the bookmark. "'Jupiter and Its Many Moons.'"

The page had a big picture of Jupiter, banded in pale oranges and pinks and even purples, almost like an Easter egg, and beneath the picture, the caption: "The planet Jupiter is more than two times larger than all the other planets put together"—something Cassie and Freddy already knew. Freddy had read this same book aloud to Grandma during those long sad days before she died, had even set up the telescope in Grandma's room, the same telescope Grandma had always set up in the one corner of their tiny overgrown backyard not dominated by the willow.

Cassie began to read. "'The biggest wonder in our solar system, in terms of size, is the planet Jupiter. The Romans named this gas giant after the principal god of Roman ...' What's that word again?" Cassie spelled the word out for Freddy, for his eyes were too weak to read in the dim light, even if he put on his big eyeglasses with the thick lenses.

"Mythology," he said.

"'... the principal god of Roman mythology.'"

Freddy interrupted. "Grandma said of all the wonders of the universe, the biggest is that we are here at all. That's something to think about. Something to remember."

The tone of his voice worried Cassie; she thought that he might start crying again. Some nights were like that, and no amount of reading could get him to stop.

She barreled onward. "Jupiter has 11 moons that we know of, but astronomers are certain many more orbit this gas giant. Its largest is Ganymede ...'" She felt proud of herself for remembering how to pronounce the moon's name, and pointed at the picture of it: a tiny black spot compared with the planet. But Freddy, although looking at the picture, could not be distracted from his train of thought.

"It's like a big gift," Freddy said.

"What is? Ganymede?"

"No. Being here. On earth."

She sighed and attempted to start reading again. But he continued.

"A wonderful gift. But one we can't keep forever. Like a balloon."

His mention of a balloon caught her off guard. She'd had a balloon once. She and Freddy had ridden the trolley to Santa Monica Pier where he had bought her a red one, but it flew away when they went on the Ferris wheel. She frowned. "I hated losing my balloon."

"Yes, but your balloon was lucky. Think about it, flying up to space like that."

"No." She shook her head and her eyes teared up as she remembered the balloon, and how it had sailed away without caring how much she loved it.

Freddy nudged her with his shoulder. "Yes, it was lucky. Really it was. It got to float all the way up to the sky. I bet it got to visit everything we see in Grandma's books. The moon and the asteroids. Mars and Venus."

"And boring old Mercury?" She didn't like that idea, her poor balloon circling around a big stupid rock.

"Mercury, too. But that's not all."

His voice had become more storyteller-like, less sad, and she decided to stop fussing about the balloon and encourage him. "What else then? The sun?"

"Maybe the sun, but I bet the balloon didn't want to get too close to that."

She imagined the balloon with its silver string, wilting near the sun, and she began to feel sad again. "And Jupiter?" she asked quickly, to snap herself out of it.

"Of course Jupiter."

"I'd like to visit Jupiter best of all." She ran her fingertip over the picture in the book—the bands of orange, pink and purple.

"Wouldn't you want to visit Saturn?"

"I suppose so," she said. "But everyone loves Saturn 'cause of its rings. But *I* love Jupiter. It's so big and gassy. Grandma was gassy. Maybe she's on Jupiter. Could heaven be on Jupiter?"

"Maybe."

"Mother says there's no heaven." Cassie felt embarrassed saying it aloud, like it was something they had agreed not to discuss.

"Mother doesn't believe in anything. And she doesn't know everything, either." Freddy had never said this before, and for a moment Cassie was shocked to hear him say it. "No one knows for sure what happens ... you know."

"After you die." She felt bad because she knew it made him feel bad, talking about dying. She patted his hand, feeling like the older sibling, not the younger. "I want to go to Jupiter someday," she said. "Can you breathe on Jupiter?" The thought made her take a deep breath, which made her lungs feel funny and she gave a little cough.

"You don't need to breathe when you go to Jupiter," Freddy said.

"But if you could?"

"Well, I suppose the air would be sweet and rotten. Remember when the sewer line broke in the street?"

"That smelled bad."

"But you'd get used to it," he said.

Cassie's little cough had agitated her lungs so that another little cough followed, and another.

Freddy sighed. "You should go back to bed. Mother will get up soon, to make her rounds. "

"Okay."

She climbed out of bed and tucked him in like Grandma used to and kissed his forehead before tiptoeing back to her room. She lay down and looked out her window. Jupiter had moved just the tiniest bit so that it now sat atop the willow, like a Christmas star. But Jupiter was not a star at all; she knew that. The biggest planet in the solar system. The third brightest thing in the sky, after the moon and Venus, and she liked how Jupiter was so big and yet not a show-off.

She coughed again, this time harder and longer. She hated when the coughing started.

When Mother came in to give Cassie her medicine, Jupiter still sat atop the tree, but four hours later, when the coughing started up again and Mother came back, Jupiter was out of sight.

Cassie fell back asleep. Jupiter, meanwhile, continued through the cold, vast blackness of space as it journeyed around the sun. The weeks passed, and then the months, while Jupiter—stormy and turbulent, unaware of those passing weeks and months—continued on the path set out for it.

One night, the sun had only just set when Jupiter winked at Cassie through the window. But she didn't notice. Her ventilator mask blocked her view.

Freddy saw it, though, and he told her how Jupiter shimmered in the pearl-like sky. His lips were against her ear, his voice louder even than their mother's. Louder even than the ventilator. Freddy's voice, the only thing Cassie heard: "The light—when you see it, it's Jupiter." Over and over he said it until she did see the light, orange and pink and purple, just like Freddy said it would be, and someone up ahead called to her, and with her last great effort she tore off the mask and gulped in the sweet rotten air.

Soul Mate

He hoped she would die today and return to him. He was so tired, waiting for her, in this so-called heaven. It was only half-heaven for him, until she returned. Until then, this place—despite its golden light and sweet aroma, despite its steady 72 degrees—didn't seem heavenly at all. Just crowded. Packed with soul mates, reuniting. All around him, the other soul mates crooned, sighed and moaned as their wounds healed and they became whole. Hearing them, seeing them—it all made his loneliness that much harder to bear. To make matters worse, the others pushed and jostled him, without apology.

He maneuvered his way through the crowd until he reached the edge of the heavenly sphere and gazed down at the blue-white orb that, until recently, had been his home and was still hers. Waiting for her to return was particularly lonely this time. It was always like that, when their lives hadn't connected. His most recent incarnation, as Jeff D. Karnes (what did the "D" stand for?—he was starting to forget these things), had been one of the worst in that sense. He saw his soul mate nearly every day, and yet they had never touched. Never talked. Never even made eye contact.

Circumstances had conspired against them, he thought, and then he laughed aloud, causing the other soul mates pressing against him to jerk away momentarily. Conspiring circumstances? No. The truth of it: She had scared Jeff D. Karnes, with her ragged clothes and matted hair. And being afraid, he could not love her. He could not love someone so obviously lost, so cut off from the world. "Love"—he laughed at himself again. He had not even come close to loving her. When he had walked the earth as Jeff D. Karnes and encountered his own true love, his eternal soul mate, he could barely even stand to look at her. Instead, he would avert his eyes and think "poor gal," or "dear god," or "where's her family?"

"You know what she will say when she returns." It was the Assistant Director—the AD—not a presence he could see, just a sweet quiet voice in his ear. Sometimes when he was waiting for his soul mate, the AD would talk to him to keep him company.

"Yes," he said, "I know what she will say. She will say 'You must be braver next time.'"

No response. The AD had moved on or else was just letting his own words sink in.

You must be braver next time—yes, his true love had said that before, and more than once. She had said it not so long ago, after their lives as two girls from the same village near Smolensk. Her as Klara, him as Lisle. He didn't usually remember what their names had been when they walked the earth, but he did when the life ended badly. And that one most certainly had. At the end, Klara and Lisle had clung together in a root cellar as that nasty little man (Neapolitan, he thought at first, but then remembered) Napoleon and his awful soldiers scourged their village, burning, raping, and killing as they went. Lisle had not lived much longer after that: She had swallowed rat poison and died in the root cellar before the soldiers could find her. But Klara, she had made it through and lived on—not much longer, true, but long enough to see soldiers die at her own hand. She sold them poisoned apples as they made their long cold retreat. They caught her at it and slashed her throat. He had watched that part from here, from this half-heaven, and when she returned, she had said, "You should have stayed alive," and "It was great fun, killing those bastards," and, of course, "You must be braver next time."

"Were you braver this time?" the AD whispered, and he had to shake his head. In his most recent life, as Jeff D. Karnes, he had not been brave at all. He had not been brave enough to bring her into his life, or to step into hers, and yet he could not keep away. As Jeff D. Karnes, he saw his true love on his lunch hour runs after the—(for a moment he couldn't remember what it was called. "The daily call," that was it.)—After the daily call with his boss, he would go on a run at Griffith Park, never anywhere else. Every day at lunch and even on weekends (his studio apartment was just across the street from the park, with a big window looking out toward it), he ran the park trails. He did not know then why he did so, but it was all so obvious now. Despite all the conspiring circumstances, the scared little heart beating in Jeff D. Karnes' chest had yearned to be with her.

He wiped condensation from the skin of the heavenly sphere and focused on the spot where she lived: the brown and green hills, the massive oaks, the dusty trails, and the most precious thing of all to him—the black tarp draped across a row of shrubs that protected her little hovel. Maybe she would crawl out today.

Or maybe she wouldn't. He hoped she wouldn't; he hoped …

"It's usually like this, isn't it?" the AD asked. "You waiting for her? And not the other way around."

He had to nod at that. "She likes to linger in the world."

The AD kept silent for a while and then said, "Funny, isn't it, how she's always crawling out of places."

It was true. He had stood at this very spot in the heavenly sphere and seen her crawl from a root cellar, her skirt full of poisoned apples; from a mine, covered in coal dust; from a trench, wearing a gas mask. And this time: from her hovel behind the shrubs.

When he was still Jeff D. Karnes, sometimes she surprised him when she emerged. He would be running along listening to his—

(what was it called? he wondered, and then it came to him)—his iPod, and suddenly there she'd be, always in the same loose and soiled clothing (an old gray pea coat, army pants, worn-out boots), her long black hair thick and tangled.

"That was all you noticed about her," the AD said, sounding terribly sad. "You didn't even notice the color of her eyes."

He knew more about her constant companion, the little gray mutt. "Her dog's eyes were black," he said, partly to the AD, partly to himself. The dog was a friendly thing, always wagging its tail when Jeff D. Karnes approached, looking up at him, so trusting, so honest, and once it had even rolled onto its back, begging for a belly scratch. Not once had he kneeled to scratch the dog's belly or pat its dirty little head. He had stayed away from the dog, not wanting to interact with its owner.

"You should have stopped to talk to the dog, if not to her."

But he never had. Circumstances had conspired to make his heart hard.

"What were those circumstances you keep on about?" the AD prodded, but he could barely remember them—the parents, the siblings, the friends. The schooling, and then the first job, and the second, and the third. Jeff D. Karnes—maybe the "D" stood for "discontented," he thought now, because that was what he was.

What a miserable life he'd had! Living alone. Running at lunch time. He would add it to his list of failed lifetimes. Maybe even worse than the life before this one, when he lived in the great tundra. That time, she had come into the world just as he did, but it took more than 15 years for them to meet, and then she had turned up as Banak, a boy in a band of wanderers—nomads who followed the tuktu herds. "Come with me," Banak had said to him. But he had not gone, he had watched Banak the nomad boy trek across the barren land until there was nothing more to see. He had lived long after, nearly 100 years in total, with children and grandchildren to attend to, but lonely all the same.

But when that life ended, she was not waiting for him in heaven. He'd had to wait for her! (He waited for the AD to bring that up, but it was an awkward point that no one, not even the AD, apparently, liked to broach.) And when she finally *did* return, she confessed that she had lived two other lifetimes while he wasted away in the tundra. "I got bored, waiting," was all she said. And so, he learned that, while he had hunted whale and patched canoes, she had killed her share of Tommies and doughboys, and later, as he had watched his children and then his grandchildren start their own families, she had traveled muddy jungle trails, preaching peace in long saffron robes. "I can't just sit around waiting for you," she had said, but with a laugh and kiss, and then they had reunited, bathed in the sweet golden light, and half-heaven became all heaven.

The AD woke him from his reverie. "She always needs a mission. That's what spurs her on."

"The dog is what's keeping her going in this incarnation," he said. "But now the dog is gone." For the past few days, whenever his own true love emerged, she did so alone, no dog in sight, and only to quickly scrounge through the trash cans, picking out old bags of potato chips and small milk cartons, before disappearing behind the shrubs again.

The dog was dead, most likely. And now she had nothing left to live for. Surely she must be ready to return to him. He saw a rustling in the shrubs and felt giddy. Maybe today she will commit suicide, he thought, just like Jeff D. Karnes did.

She emerged, brushing leaves and twigs from the same loose clothing she always wore. When she returned to him, he would ask about the conspiring circumstances, and how she had ended up living behind a shrub in Griffith Park—alone, dejected, an outcast…

The AD gasped, and that's when he saw it. She was not alone. The dog was not dead after all. It trotted alongside her, its tail wagging, its ears perked up. Behind the dog trailed a string of puppies, tripping and scampering over their fat little paws.

She would not be returning to him anytime soon, he saw that now. "No need to cry," the AD said, but it was too late. The reunited souls surrounding him did not even notice his sobs, but she stopped and looked up at the sudden downpour. She looked up and let the rain kiss her face.

Monster on the Loose

To be out of the attic for just a little while. It is all you think of, each long, lonely day. Midnight is the best time for it. By then, the doctor has finished his notes, smoked his second bowl of opium, and is asleep in the armchair near the fire.

The kitchen door at the back of the house is your means of escape. It is barred with a deadbolt, but the doctor doesn't know you have found the key and have learned to use it. Not easy to use, a key, with hands like yours, but you have practiced, and now it takes only seconds to get out.

No one appears to be out at this time, except you. Not even the three-legged cat that lives across the way, amid the broken glass and crumbling brick. Perhaps it is nursing its newest batch of kittens. You have seen the kittens through your attic window. They look like the little powdered pastries the doctor dunks in his tea.

The gas lights flicker. The street glows yellow. You move carefully, quietly, staying in the shadows, under branches of dying elms. The abandoned houses lining the street look even more forsaken than during the day. How you would love to walk in the sun! But it is unthinkable. Impossible. No one can know about you. The doctor is very clear about that.

Far down the street, where the gas lights burn bright, someone is walking. A smallish person, but one who walks with confidence. One with a job to do.

You stand against a tree and watch the person approach. A boy. A teenage boy. The worst kind of person, from what you know about the world.

The boy reaches the corner but doesn't turn. He is close enough now that you can see his chopped yellow hair, his mouth so full of teeth he cannot seem to keep it closed. You have seen this boy before. You have seen him throw rocks at the three-legged cat. You have seen the other batch of kittens, the one before this, disappear into his burlap bag. The three-legged cat meowed as the kittens struggled and squirmed to escape and, because you could not help yourself, you began to moan, soon so loud that the boy looked up at your window high up in the attic, and the doctor ran in and gave you the draught that makes you sleep.

The boy continues toward you, burlap bag in hand. It is empty now, but not for long. You have melded yourself against the tree, lungs collapsed, until you are nearly invisible. The boy's face glows in the light. His eyes are dark pits.

He is near you now, only feet away. He shakes open the burlap bag. It gapes black and deep, and you can smell the inside. The smell of kitten, mixed with something else. Something rotten and moldy and stale. Like water trapped in a basement.

You step away from the tree. You block the boy's path. Your neck frill spreads wide and, before he can scream, you have sprayed him with the sticky muck that will burn him clean away. He turns and runs, wailing the wail of your mother the day she saw you. He drops the bag as the skin falls off. The charred bones blacken and collapse into a pile of dust.

The street is quiet again as you turn toward home. You bow your head, like praying. The scales on your feet shimmer silver with moonlight.

The Dolphin and the Healer King

The city aquarium had only one dolphin left in its tank, a fat old female named Big Gal. She was lonely most of the time, with her only regular company being the seagulls (who yakked on and on about the deplorable lack of french fries), so Big Gal was always happy to see Henry arrive for his weekly visit. She clucked in an affectionate, motherly way whenever she saw Henry waddling toward the tank, a squat little man with hardly any hair, carrying a soiled paper bag. She liked his company and the stinky fish he tossed her way, and, maybe most of all, she liked the stories he told.

Today as usual she swam to the edge of the tank to greet him, and he dropped an anchovy into her mouth. "It's like this," he said, which is what he always said first thing. But then: "My wife wants to replace the floors with hardwood."

Big Gal cackled sympathetically. Poor Henry—there was always some new project his wife wanted done. Today it was the floors that needed replacing. Last week it was the pipes, and before that the bathtubs (there were three) and the windows. Big Gal circled the tank and then, to cheer him, she flew up in the air and did a back flip. Henry doled out an extra portion of stinky fish for her effort.

"*All* the floors," Henry said, shaking his head. "But what can I do? She's my sweetheart, Big Gal. I want her to be happy." His smile was wistful and full of longing. "Still," and here he sighed, "every darn room."

Big Gal nuzzled his hand. Henry caressed her snout and continued.

"'*Are you sure, dear? The Pergo looks so nice—*' That's what I said to her. '*But, dear, Pergo doesn't have the same energy as real wood*'—that's what she said in return. Oh well, oh well. We must keep peace in our own little kingdoms, mustn't we, no matter the cost. It will all work out in the end, I suppose. Yes, it will all work out in the end."

Big Gal propelled herself upright and planted a delicate little kiss on Henry's clean-shaven cheek. She understood his predicament perfectly. She couldn't understand all the words from his mouth, but she could feel his thoughts, and from there she could gather what his words meant, and she felt how much he loved his wife and how this love helped him accept all the changes (although the *expense*—that was another thing entirely), and deeper still she saw in Henry's mind's eye the transformation of his home as he met his wife's demands.

She saw the corroded and rusty pipes, spewing all manner of gunk, replaced with new coppery ones, as shiny and smooth as tropical eels; the small tanks he called bathtubs ripped out and the new ones installed and filled with steaming, gleaming water; and the cloudy, cracked window glass removed and replaced with shiny panes that sparkled like sunlight on water.

Despite her sympathy for poor Henry, Big Gal liked seeing his house transform, and she was eager to see how it all turned out. But the hardwood project was the last one she would hear about.

That very night, a crew of men with a net, a crane, and a tanker truck came to the aquarium to take Big Gal back to the ocean. She resisted at first. Life at the aquarium had been boring, true, and constricted, but at least she was safe and also free from the social conventions of the dolphin world. She evaded the men as best she could, swimming just out of their reach, and causing at least two of them to say "shit" and "goddamn" more than once. But men with nets usually don't give up, and these men were no different, and it all ended with Big Gal deposited into the tanker truck. "Back to the wild," one of the men said at the very end as she slid into the ocean, but she swished her tail at that. *The wild*, she thought. *There's nothing wild about it.* The dolphin world is a highly structured one, you see, and Big Gal worried about finding her place in it.

And indeed, once she found a pod to join, the other dolphins immediately asked her to choose a role. "No lollygaggers," they all told her, with even the littlest pups chiming in on that score. And so, after careful consideration, and knowing she had no skill whatsoever in maneuvering, scouting, clowning, or negotiating (the only other jobs the pod had open at the time), she decided to become the pod storyteller, as the previous one had recently disappeared into a tuna net.

But living all those years alone at the aquarium hadn't left her with much material.

"There was a man named Henry who brought me stinky fish once a week and spent all his money fixing up his house, just to please his wife. It all started one day when a baseball broke a window ..."

The story failed completely. The others in her pod didn't care about any of it. "Who is this Henry?" "Why should we care about him?" "Or his wife?" "Or his window?" After that, she heard more than one of them mutter "lollygagger" whenever she swam by.

This was a truly worrisome position for her to be in—new to the pod, with a value-add edging quickly toward the negative. At any moment, she knew, she could be exiled. She'd seen it happen before. Long ago, before her stint at the aquarium, her Uncle Murray had been exiled. Why? For failing to spot a tricky stretch of kelp during a scouting venture. The pod exiled him, and off he went, his tail swishing back and forth in a despondent kind of way. And after that, no one was allowed to speak his name.

And this was to be her fate? She, who had survived all that time alone in the aquarium tank, who had somehow kept her spirits up, who had not gone tank-crazy like so many others had, those poor wretches who scraped themselves against the sides until they bled; she, who had survived all that, would be exiled?

Hell no.

If the pod didn't care about Henry, well then, she would find a way to *make* them care. She swam in circles until she had worked it out:

Henry was not just a man, but a hero …

A hero who sacrificed his own happiness to please his wife …

Better yet, Henry was a king who repaired his castle to please his queen …

Better yet still: Henry was a Healer King who … who repaired his castle … not only to please his queen, but … but to heal his kingdom.

Dolphins appreciated that kind of thing, Big Gal knew, because their own kingdom needed healing. The kingdom of the sea had long been rife with strife and disharmony, what with the centuries-long war between the dolphins and the porpoises, a war that had disrupted even the deepest darkest part of the sea (because even there everyone knew your pro-dolphin or pro-porpoise stance).

At the next story time, she started this way:

"Once there was a king who lived in a kingdom torn apart by strife and disharmony."

That immediately caught the pod's attention.

"His queen cried and moaned, and she pleaded with the king and said the problem was the castle: if it could be repaired, the kingdom would be healed."

Big Gal saw the elder members of the pod glance at each other. "An allegory, that's what this is," a cow whispered to a bull.

Their piqued interest encouraged Big Gal, and she continued. "The queen took the king's hand and said, 'The windows of the castle must be replaced ...'"

The whole pod groaned at that—they had heard enough about windows, and about the bipeds who lived on land.

"I bet now she'll bring up the baseball," one of the pups complained, and the others laughed.

But Big Gal had prepared herself for this and hurried on:

"The windows are cloudy and cracked, my lord. Without clear sight into the kingdom, how can we ever hope to heal it?"

A collective gasp and whispers of "allegory," "allegory" spread among them, even among the pups, and Big Gal knew she had scored in a big way. She had been locked up in a tank for years, true, but she knew not only that all dolphins long for peace in the sea, but also that they all love allegory.

Scholars have long pondered this love of allegory in the dolphin world, but consider this: Dolphins have the brightest minds of all Earth's creatures (and here our porpoise friends will roll their eyes, no doubt), and bright minds are constantly in search of the deeper meaning in things. Such minds are drawn to allegorical puzzles, just as catfish are drawn to hooks baited with orange cheese. "What can it mean?" one dolphin will ask another, and before you know it, they have solved the puzzle and, of course, will let everyone know about it (with typical dolphin arrogance, as any porpoise is sure to tell you).

Happily for our heroine, Big Gal had a knack for turning stories into allegories. Poor old Henry, who had fussed so over his hardwood dilemma, became a Healer King in the dolphin world— one who tore out the old foundation of his castle and replaced it with stronger material.

"And thus, with firmer footing, he felt more confident, which in turn eased the minds of all his subjects, who thought, 'Now here is a man who knows how to rule!' But he didn't stop there. With a wave of his trident, the Healer King dismantled all the rusty old pipes that poured foul, polluted water into the kingdom and replaced them with sparkling new pipes that flushed away all impurities. With the flow of fresh water now secured, he destroyed the cracked and rotting bathing tanks and replaced them with tubs that gleamed like abalone shells, where he soaked and pondered all the other good he would do."

On and on Big Gal went, making up new tales when she ran out of Henry material, and the pod seemed to like each story better than the last, and they always cheered whenever she got to the end and said, "And in this way, by healing his own home, the Healer King brought peace to the kingdom."

Her stories began to spread, and soon dolphins everywhere knew about Henry the Healer King. Many a dolphin thought, "I, too, can heal the kingdom," and in this way the collective attitude began to change—become more positive, as it were. And soon, more quickly than you'd think, the ocean again became a place of peace. The war between the dolphins and the porpoises came quietly and thankfully to an end, and, more importantly to our own story, Big Gal's place in the pod was secured.

Henry never knew any of this, of course. Instead, he toiled on, day in, day out, doling out money like there was no tomorrow, forever worrying that the new pipes were not 100% copper. "And I think I paid too much for the granite countertops," he told the seals, who barked sympathetically and clapped as he tossed them more fish.

Beyond the Fence

Mr. Wolfe didn't tell Kate much about this particular job before sending her out. "Old guy at Woodside, just about dead," he said, pouring himself a Scotch, even though it wasn't yet noon. "Basic processing. BTF." Kate hoped the man would die before she got there. That would make her sad job a little easier. But now, here at Woodside Nursing Home, Kate saw he was still alive. Hardly breathing, nothing but a lump under a thin gray blanket, but still alive. Which explained the photograph propped up on the nightstand.

In these types of cases (BTF—when the dying would be planted beyond the fence), any personal effects were thrown out as soon as the person died. This made it less complicated for Forever Tree seed sellers like Kate. This helped the seed seller forget that this was a human being lying here, one with a history. Easier to plant someone beyond the fence that way. But get a glimpse of any kind of personal effect and, as Mr. Wolfe liked to say, "You could end up watering a person for the next 50 years."

Kate was about to grab the photo and stuff it into the briefcase strapped over her shoulder when the nurse marched in. She was an old woman, probably around 40, Kate guessed. Anyone over 35 seemed ancient these days. Kate had 10 more years before she fell into that group. Ten more years—the time stretched before her like a prison sentence.

The nurse gave Kate a quick glance as she picked up the chart lying at the man's feet. "Basic processing," she said, making notes and checking boxes. "BTF."

The man on the bed opened his eyes. *BTF*—he knew what that meant. Everyone did. His soul would still be poured into a Forever Tree seed, but instead of being planted alongside anyone he knew in a Forever Forest, he'd go beyond the fence. Alone forever.

The man didn't look up at Kate, even though she stood right at his bedside. He stared at the floor and, after a moment, huddled into a fetal position. Her boss Mr. Wolfe called it "the hug of the dead." An apt name for it, really, Kate thought, since so many of the dead ended up that way. During the summer when the plagues came around, most corpses scattered everywhere were coiled like that, in the hug of the dead. Kate had counted 15 in the Dunkin' Donuts parking lot last summer, their faces covered in flu smear, while men in hazmat suits loaded them into white trucks.

The last one they loaded in: Mr. Skeffington, her next-door neighbor. She hadn't even known he was sick, but that was how fast the plague bug could take you. So fast you didn't even have time to have your soul gene extracted. "The gene expresses a few minutes after death, when it's getting ready to depart," Mr. Wolfe had said, her first day on the job. "You gotta extract the DNA then, Kate, and there's no time to tarry. No wishing you were someplace else, doing something else."

The briefcase strap dug deep into Kate's shoulder, heavy with seed catalogs. The man in bed before her still hadn't looked up, but she could see now that his eyes were clear and bright, unclouded by cataracts. Early 60s, she thought; maybe even late 50s. His eyes were a deep brown, so brown that the whites around the irises looked almost blue. Eyes like her Uncle Jack's. "Uncle Jack," she'd say, sitting on his lap, long long ago, Sunday pot roast and mashed potatoes cooking in the kitchen. "Uncle Jack, your whites are all blue."

She slid the strap off her shoulder and set the briefcase on the floor. "Does he have a tree preference?"

"Not that I know of," the nurse said, still engrossed in her paperwork. "Hasn't said a word since he got here."

Kate had met such people before. The people in the photo—the one she wouldn't let herself look at—were probably his family, and they were probably all dead now, Kate thought, all except him. He was the only survivor, somehow untouched by the plague bug, and left to live the rest of his life alone. Such people often ended up like he did, wandering the streets, speechless and dazed, and picked up from the gutter and brought to a place like this to die and have their DNA extracted. Other lone survivors, like Kate, like Mr. Wolfe, hadn't gone that route. They went to work every day instead. They drank their lunches alone and went home to quiet houses.

Kate sat down on the folding chair beside the bed. "I'll sit here awhile, if you don't mind."

"Suit yourself." The nurse set down the chart at the foot of the bed and left the room.

The routine in these types of cases, when the customer was a "nonresponsive," was to choose an elm and be done with it. Sign the paperwork and move on. That is what Mr. Wolfe would tell her to do. He had said it plenty of times. "No need to give them the spiel, Kate. E-L-M. That's all there is to it."

If it were up to her, people could have a choice about the whole thing. If it were up to her, people wouldn't be forced to graft their souls onto Forever Seeds if they didn't want to. But the law said otherwise, and she could go to jail if she didn't soul-extract this man. The United States of Forever Trees, Inc., Kate thought. That's what the country had become.

So Kate had sold more than her share of elm seeds, and every night on her drive home she saw the trees they had become. Lonely, ragged-looking things, planted beside dumpsters, in abandoned lots, and on the edge of landfills; all of them slow-growing, and none more than 10 feet high, as if getting that tall was all they could muster, their leaves more yellow than green, since no one watered them or fed them Everlife Fertilizer.

And this man would be another. Soon she would drive by him, too, and someday she would forget which one he was, and no one on earth would remember him then.

"E-L-M, Kate," Mr. Wolfe's voice sang in her head, and still she sat there, not able to do it, and decided finally that at least she could let this man choose his tree. Just because he'd be planted beyond the fence, she reasoned, didn't mean he couldn't choose his tree.

But she didn't know how to start. She cleared her throat and put the briefcase on her lap, but the man just stared at the floor and wouldn't look at her. The room was cold and quiet, and the only light came from the small lamp on the nightstand. Kate wrapped her sweater closer around her. This place must be full of the dead, she thought, with corpses coiled in every bed.

She waited in the quiet, and after a while, the man slowly moved his gaze toward the photo on the nightstand. His expression softened, and his whole body seemed to relax as he regarded it. She told herself not to look at it, and Mr. Wolfe's voice in her head told her not to as well, and that she had to stay strong in these types of cases, and reminded her about the whole "watering a person for 50 years" scenario, but the photo was like a living thing. It tapped on her shoulder, coughed politely and whispered in her ear, wanting her attention. She was looking at it before she could stop herself.

The picture showed a group of people. Smiling people, every one. They sat at a picnic table under a weeping willow, and there was a lake or river in the background. A happy summer day, from the looks of it. She picked out the man right away. There he was with a little girl on his lap, a little girl with bright golden hair ...

She turned away again. *These kinds of cases, they'll break your heart if you let them*—another thing Mr. Wolfe liked to say, but never in the morning. Always toward the end of the day, when the bottle of Scotch was near its end.

The harder she tried not to think of the photo, the more it came to life, and then, dreamlike, it turned into *her* family sitting there at the table, with their easy laughter and gentle teasing. There they were, picnicking on the Delaware River on the 4th of July, her favorite day of the year. There was Aunt Dor, dishing red Jell-O salad from a big white Tupperware, and Uncle Jack next to her, sipping on a Budweiser, his arm draped around her shoulder. And Mom and Dad, they were there, too: Dad at the end of the table, manning the hot dog grill, tongs in one hand, cigarette in the other, and Mom, her head tilted back, eyes closed, laughing at one of his jokes ("Oh, Ned, you're awful. Awful!"). But where were the children? Where were Kate, her cousins, her brother Max? Where were they? Down at the river, of course. Swinging from a rope tied to the big black birch alongside the river. Jumping into the swirling green water. "Watch me, Katie, watch me!" That's what Max cried, every time he swung.

But those days were long past. The plagues had come and changed everything. Within a week, Kate's family was gone. Dying in a summer plague, before the discovery of the soul gene and the planting of the Forever Forests. Her brother Max was the last to go. Just barely a man when he died, not even 18. He'd never even had a girlfriend. "You were always the lucky one, Katie"—that was the last thing he said. It was hard hearing anything in that big hospital tent full of the sick, so she had leaned closer to his cot to hear him. He reached out then, to touch the mask over her mouth, but she had jolted away.

She shifted in her chair and sighed. Mr. Wolfe was right. It didn't help to think of these things. His voice had been silent in her head, but now it came back strong and clear. "Focus on the work,

Kate. The work. That's the important thing now." She took out a catalog from her briefcase and started her sales pitch.

"We have a wide choice of seeds. Everything from crepe myrtle to dogwood, Lebanon cedar to redwood." She flipped through the catalog, hoping to catch the man's eye. "Deciduous or evergreen, that's the first thing to decide. I'm sure you know the difference between the two." No reaction, so she barreled ahead. "It all depends on how active you want to be, once you cross over. You want to stay active, I'd suggest going the deciduous route. A flowering pear or a maple. You want to be more reflective, I'd go evergreen. Oak is our most popular."

At the word "oak," the man finally raised his eyes and looked at her. Some people were like that. Mention a hundred different trees and they'd say "no" to all of them, and then suddenly the right one came along and they perked up. Mr. Wolfe had a theory about it, like he did about everything. "Everyone has a favorite tree. Didn't you? I sure did. A big old magnolia. That's what I want to be when my time comes. Don't forget."

"The good thing about our oaks," Kate said, "is the very fast incubation period. Because of our Growth Propel Technology, you'll be fairly mature within a year. Here. Let me show you." She scooted closer to the man's bed and held up the picture of an oak with a wide canopy. He squinted to look at it. He needed a pair of glasses, Kate thought, but there were none to give him. "This is two years' growth," she said, more confident now, now that she'd drawn his attention. "Another good thing about oaks is that they're drought-tolerant ..."

She wished she hadn't reminded the man that no one would water him once he was planted. Wherever he was, Mr. Wolfe shook his head and poured himself another drink. She blushed and sat back in her chair and busied herself by flipping through the catalog.

But after a moment, the man smiled at her. His eyes lit up, too, with the tiniest of flickers, as if this whole watering thing was a little joke between them. It had been a long time since she had shared a joke with anyone. She blushed even more, feeling shy, and tried to remember how to respond.

It felt dangerous, remembering such a thing, and Mr. Wolfe clucked his disapproval in her ear. But the memory slipped back, quick and graceful, before she could stop it.

At least it's not eggplant—she and Dad used to say that to each other at the dinner table whenever Mom experimented with a new recipe ("I found it in Good Housekeeping!"). Mom's experiments turned out pretty good most times, but a few were downright disasters, including, worst of all, the eggplant parmesan, which Mom swore she had prepared just like the recipe said to, and yet the eggplant was as tough as an old boot. But Mom had worked so hard on it that Kate, Dad and Max chewed away until the whole pan was empty. Afterward, whenever Mom pushed a new dish on them, they were always glad for one thing: "At least it's not eggplant," Dad would whisper to Kate, or sometimes the other way around, and always with a laugh in their eyes.

"At least it's not eggplant," Kate said now, very, very quietly. If only Dad had been planted, she could visit him and say that, and his branches would sway and his leaves would fall gently on to her head like little soft kisses. If only. If only. *The two worst words in the English language* is what Mr. Wolfe called them. He was right. There were no if onlys. She had no trees to visit.

The man had been watching her closely, his eyes kind, the slight smile on his face more sad than happy. Kate let herself look deep into his eyes, eyes so much like Uncle Jack's, and she let him look deep into hers. They held each other in a kind of embrace that way, and for a sweet moment they were not alone.

Stiffly, slowly, he reached for the photograph. His hand shook as he did so. He had workman's hands, Kate saw now, strong and calloused. A mechanic or a plumber, she thought. Or maybe a carpenter. Her dad had been a carpenter. "Hand me the sander, will you, Katie?" he'd say, sunlight streaming through the workshop windows, sawdust glimmering in the air. "Or as we pros like to call it, 'the thing that smooths wood.'"

The man pleaded gently with his eyes, and Kate took the photo from the nightstand and handed it to him. A small wrinkled snapshot, unframed, probably kept inside his back pocket for years and years. He put the photo against his heart and held out his other hand to Kate. "Don't do it, " Mr. Wolfe said, but she took the man's hand without hesitating. Mr. Wolfe went completely mute then and shook his head, his eyes moist as he poured himself the last of the Scotch.

The man had a hand just like her dad's—and like Uncle Jack's, and her brother Max's, too, if only he'd lived long enough. She had buried their ashes on the hill behind her house. Then she put a bench there, one her dad had built, of polished oak. Most nights, after work, she sat on the bench and looked out over Forever Forest No. 23, a particularly pretty forest of maples, which turned bright red, orange and yellow in autumn, and from that spot she could listen to the contented sighs of the Planted as they relinquished their leaves to the ground.

My spot on the hill could use some shade, she thought.

My spot on the hill is just close enough for the garden hose to reach.

My spot on the hill, she thought, sitting taller, has room for an oak. For more than one oak, even. There's even room for a magnolia.

My spot on the hill could become my own little forest.

"Oak," she said, and the man smiled a little smile and closed his eyes. "We'll go with oak." And gently, very gently, when she saw it was time, she let go of his hand. She took the photo and slid it gently into her briefcase. And then, when the time was right, just as the soul gene expressed, she extracted the DNA, just as she had thousands of times before. Just like Mr. Wolfe had showed her to. From right above the heart.